A Seat at the Front

Moira Wairama

Learning Media®

When Tony caught the crosstown bus,
he liked to sit at the back. When he was
with his grandma, they always sat
at the front.

"Why do you always sit at the front of
the bus, Grandma?" Tony asked one day.

"I sit at the front because of Rosa Parks,"
she replied.

"Is she a friend of yours?" Tony asked.
Grandma smiled and shook her head.

"When I was a young girl, I lived in
a place called Montgomery, in Alabama.
In those days, there was a law that said
black people and white people weren't
allowed to sit together on the bus.
White people sat at the front of the bus,
and black people sat at the back. If the
seats at the front of the bus were full,
the black people had to stand and give
the white people their seats.

"There was a woman my mother knew
in Montgomery named Rosa Parks.
She belonged to a group of people
who thought it was wrong that black
Americans were treated differently from
white Americans.

"One day, when Rosa Parks was coming home from work, a white man got on the bus. People were sitting in all the front seats, so he moved toward the back, where Rosa was sitting. He told Rosa to give him her seat. Rosa was tired and said no. The man was angry. He told the bus driver that Rosa wouldn't give him her seat. The bus driver called the police, and Rosa Parks was arrested.

"When the black people in Montgomery heard what had happened, they were angry. They decided not to travel on the buses until black people could sit wherever they wanted. People called this a bus boycott. News of it spread around the country. Black people started protests and boycotts all over the United States."

Grandma sighed. "Not many families had cars in those days. I can still remember how sore my feet got the first week I had to walk to school. My father was luckier than me. He worked a long way from where we lived, but a white man he knew gave him a ride to work in his car. The bus boycott went on for over a year. It was a hard time for many black people. In the end, the law was changed, and black people were allowed to sit wherever they wanted on the bus."

Grandma turned her head and smiled at Tony. "That's why I like to sit at the front of the bus."

During the rest of the bus ride, Tony thought about Grandma's story. He thought that Rosa Parks would be a good subject for his next class project. He also thought that from now on, whenever he rode the bus, he too would sit at the front.